THE SUPER-NICE ARE
SUPER-ANNOYING

THINK YOU CAN HANDLE
JAMIE KELLY'S FIRST YEAR OF DIARIES?

AND DON'T MISS YEAR TWO!

Jim Benton's Tales from Mackerel Middle School

DEAR DUMB DIARY,

YEAR TWO

THE SUPER-NICE ARE SUPER-ANNOYING

BY JAMIE KELLY

SCHOLASTIC INC.

New York   Toronto   London   Auckland
Sydney   Mexico City   New Delhi   Hong Kong

ISBN 978-0-545-37763-8

Copyright © 2012 by Jim Benton

All rights reserved. Published by Scholastic Inc. SCHOLASTIC and associated logos are trademarks and/or registered trademarks of Scholastic Inc. DEAR DUMB DIARY is a registered trademark of Jim Benton.

12 11 10 9 8 7 6 5 4 3 2   12 13 14 15 16/0
Printed in the U.S.A.   40
First printing, June 2012

*For my family, who are always
paradigms of good manners
and junk.*

*Special thanks to the delicate and
well-mannered creatures of grace at
Scholastic: Shannon Penney, Anna Bloom,
Jackie Hornberger, and Yaffa Jaskoll.
And thanks to Kristen LeClerc for her
clean, polite assistance.*

IF
YOU CAN'T
ACCEPT THAT
INVITATION,

I'd like
to offer you
an invitation to
the **EMERGENCY ROOM**

PLEASE MAKE
YOUR CHOICE.

THIS DIARY PROPERTY OF:

Jamie Kelly

SCHOOL: MACKEREL MIDDLE SCHOOL

FAVORITE FOOD: ~~SPAGHETTI~~ SOMETHING ELSE

GRADES: GOOD. PRETTY GOOD. I'M TRYING.

HAIR: LIKE ~~SPAGHETTI~~ EW EW EW EW SOMETHING ELSE

Dear Whoever Is Reading My Dumb Diary,

Do you have any idea how **RUDE** you look, with your nose in somebody else's diary? What do you think we'll think of you and your nose now? We certainly won't ever invite you to smell something polite, like a bouquet of roses or an opera.

Honestly, how do you think that appears to others? Do you think that's **nice**? (And, hey, sit up straight.)

And whatever you do, don't get all super-apologetic about it now, because we find that pretty annoying as well.

Politeness Experts worldwide agree that reading somebody's diary isn't just like chewing with your mouth open, it's like chewing with your mouth open in your underpants with your bare feet in the soup bowl and a finger up your nose, and what you're chewing is a piece of raw chicken wrapped up in an old piece of notebook paper on which is written a disgusting joke in very bad handwriting.

Signed, *Jamie Kelly*

P.S. I know you should never call people names like "gross" or "disgusting" or "stupid," but I didn't call them anything. I **wrote** it. And if my parents punish me for it, I will know that they have read my diary, which would be inexcusably impolite.

SUNDAY 01

Dear Dumb Diary,

You probably don't believe that a nostril can do you harm. You're **wrong** about that.

My favorite show of all time, in addition to my other favorite shows of all time, is on TV right now. But I'm up in my room, unable to watch it because of a nostril.

I know what you're thinking, Dumb Diary. You're thinking, *Jamie, the nostrils are some of the least destructive of the head holes.*

Sure, the mouth is the most destructive head hole by far, with its ability to both bite *and* whistle songs badly, but nostrils are hazardous in ways you may not be able to imagine.

Also, Dumb Diary, you're probably thinking something about how nice my eyes look tonight. **Kisses!**

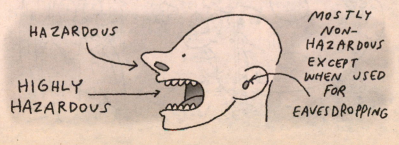

HAZARDOUS

HIGHLY HAZARDOUS

MOSTLY NON-HAZARDOUS EXCEPT WHEN USED FOR EAVESDROPPING

Oh, Dumb Diary, you have SO much to learn about nostrils. You know a lot about eyes and how nice they can look, but you'd get a C in nostrils.

And since we're discussing the subject of getting something in nostrils, let me tell you about Friday. I'll tell you in the least horrible way I can:

At lunch, Pinsetti laughed until a spaghetti noodle **came out his nose**. It just dangled there for a moment, and it was incredibly disgusting, but I also found myself staring at it, imagining for a moment that maybe a mouse was preparing to descend a tiny rope.

Isabella, who has mean older brothers and therefore no longer reacts to the brain chemical that causes **disgust** to occur, reached over, slowly drew the entire spaghetti noodle out of Pinsetti's nostril, and laid it gently on the back of my unsuspecting hand.

why did I think this might happen?

Two thoughts race through your head at a moment like this. The first one is:

EEEEEEEEEEEEEEEEEEEEWWWWWWWW!

While it's true that the pasta entered Pinsetti's mouth as spaghetti, and spaghetti — even cafeteria spaghetti — is one of my all-time favorite foods, once an object exits through a nostril, it is transformed into booger. This is just science, plain and simple. It works for anything. Put a raisin into your nose for even **one second**, then pull it back out, and it becomes booger.

Look, if you don't believe me, why don't you go ahead and eat that raisin?

You won't: It's booger now.

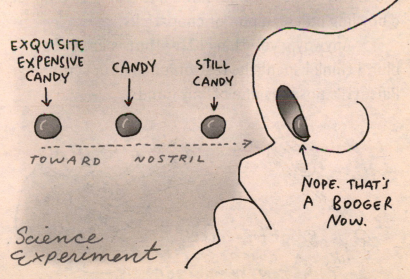

EXQUISITE EXPENSIVE CANDY

CANDY

STILL CANDY

TOWARD   NOSTRIL

NOPE. THAT'S A BOOGER NOW.

Science Experiment

The second thought that goes through your head at a moment like this is: I bet I can fly upward and backward, away from this spaghetti noodle, just by flapping my arms in a panic.

Nobody can really fly, of course, but that won't stop you from trying. All that you'll really do is shoot backward out of your chair hard enough to crash into the cafeteria monitor, Miss Bruntford. This will send her **toppling over**, causing her to make the sound of a meteor hitting the Earth, if the meteor was made out of an enormous mass of very wet ham.

I'm not saying any of this was her fault, but let's face it: She **is** expecting a little much from those tiny heels she wears. It's like trying to balance a bowling ball on a pair of chopsticks.

Anyway, everything after that is kind of a blur. I think I spent the rest of lunch hour scrubbing Pinsetti's nose residue off my hand.

Bruntford feels like a couch stuffed with raw hamburger

Of course, Dad made spaghetti for dinner tonight, which normally would be a huge relief, because **ANYTHING OTHER THAN MOM'S COOKING** is one of my favorite foods. But even though I really wanted to eat it, **I couldn't**. Because now, for me, spaghetti isn't spaghetti anymore. Now spaghetti is a product of Pinsetti's nostril.

We got into an argument about dinner, and I got sent to my room. I may have referred to the meal as booger without explaining what happened on Friday, and I may have screamed it, and I may have shoved the plate away from me, and I may have screamed it a few more times.

So I'm missing my TV show. I blame Pinsetti's nostril, and somehow I feel that Isabella may have to share some of the blame as well.

But it's easy to misunderstand Isabella. Once when I thought she had stolen my dessert, she explained that it was just something called **SURPRISE SHARING**.

MONDAY 02

Dear Dumb Diary,

    I have mostly all new teachers this year. This is because teachers only learn enough to teach up to a certain level. See, third-grade math teachers can't even **do** fourth-grade math. They only learn it up to a third-grade level, so that's what they teach, and that's why you have to keep getting new teachers.

    Think about it: Kindergarten teachers probably can't even go the bathroom by themselves.

Preschool teachers actually sign their checks with fingerpaint.

My new social studies teacher is Mr. Smith. I know that sounds like a fake name, but if you had to choose a fake name, would you choose Smith? Everybody would know it was a fake. It's so obvious that Smith is a fake name that the people who say that their name is Smith are the only ones that are, for sure, telling the truth.

Besides, we don't have any reason to believe he's using a fake name.

Except that he's wearing a wig.

Don't look at it. Don't look at it.

When a man wears a wig, it's customary to call it a toupee, because calling it something in a foreign language is supposed to make it look less ridiculous.

For **this** toupee to look less ridiculous, he'd also have to actually wear it in that foreign country.

Where we couldn't see him.

unconvincing hairlike fibers

real head hair struggling to peek out

not the same color as the rest of his hair

smells like Barbie hair

I don't think men need to worry about their hair that much. Many attractive individuals are bald, like,

Um
Homer Simpson and

Um
Voldemort and

Um
My big toe.

 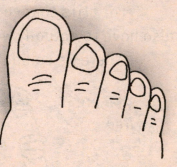

Okay, Mr. Smith. Keep the toupee. Maybe you can see if they manufacture smiles that you could wear as well.

Dumb Diary, like most people, I **hate** the alphabet. Mostly because I can't alphabetize things unless I sing part of the alphabet song in my head when I'm doing it, and people can tell I'm doing that because it makes me bob my head a little.

This came up today because Mr. Smith has us starting a unit on how people in other cultures approach different issues. We do a lot of projects in groups at my school now, because they say it's great preparation for the **real world**. This is because projects often go wrong in the real world, and so we need to learn how to swiftly blame things on somebody else nearby.

you aren't really an adult until you can blame well.

Today, surprisingly, for the first time ever, the alphabet ACTUALLY HELPED SOMEBODY when it had to acknowledge that *J* (for Jamie) was pretty close to *H* (for Hudson Rivers, eighth-cutest boy in my grade). Because Mr. Smith was choosing teams alphabetically by first names, he put us together for the project.

A very, very long time ago — like **months** — being paired with Hudson would have made it difficult for me to breathe. But I'm older now, and quite a sophisticated young lady at that, so all it did was make me sweat my pits off.

I know what you're saying, Dumb Diary. You're saying, "Where was Isabella when this happened?"

How many times have I heard that exact question?

Answer: She was down in the principal's office. Lately, the principal has been talking to Isabella **before** she does anything wrong. He likes to guess what she might do next. I've been doing this for years. It's kind of fun.

The Situation	What I guess she'll do...
Talking Bear walks in!!	Knocks Bear out. Goes through his pockets.
Aliens invade Earth!	Teams up with Aliens, co-owns Earth.
Giant spiders EAT people!	Actually I think she'd be cool with that.

If Isabella hadn't been down at the principal's office, she would have been paired with Hudson, because, of course, Isabella's name begins with *I*. This is really appropriate since most of her sentences do, too:

"I want that."

"I will mess you up."

"I didn't wipe insect remains on that."

But she wasn't in the room and I was, so I was paired with Hudson. When she got back, Isabella was paired up with Yolanda, who is one of the **dainty people**.

Do you know the type of person I mean? These people are nice, with small, thin, clean necks and tiny clean fingers that are just right for holding perfect, clean little sandwiches and clean, fragile ceramic objects. Nobody has a problem with the dainty — they're never loud, and they never argue. I would draw Yolanda here, but I can't remember exactly what she looks like, just that she's massively dainty. I'll remember more tomorrow.

When Isabella returned, she didn't really care much that she didn't get paired up with Hudson. She's really great like that. Isabella can work well with anybody who is doing all of the work.

Oh, and one other thing. Mr. Smith made Angeline partners with Mike Pinsetti. And it turns out that Mike is his *middle name.* (Something revealed on this year's attendance lists.) His first name is actually Antonio, but Isabella said that since every male in his family is named Antonio, lots of them go by their middle names. Isn't that interesting?

No. Not really.

ANTONIO MICHAEL
(PINSETTI)

ANTONIO BONIO

MICRO ANTONIO

ANTONIO UNICORNIO

ANTONIO PONIO

FRED
(ADOPTED)

ANTONIO WHATEVERO

Of course, this isn't **ALL** good news. I did really bad on the last social studies project — like, **SUPER AWFUL** bad. I was teamed up with Isabella. Our project was about Pilgrims, and Isabella put in a whole bunch of research she did about them dressing in black because they were ninjas.

Yeah, guess what. They weren't. I failed.

That's how these group projects work. Somebody lied to Isabella about those ninjas, and we **both** had to pay for it.

A lot more is riding on this grade, though, so I really have to nail this project.

Lies they told Isabella

Pilgrims were Ninjas!

They were chased out of Europe by Bigfoots!

This made them so mad they karate chopped Plymouth rock in HALF!

TUESDAY 03

Dear Dumb Diary,

Today at lunch, Angeline was nicely circulating a nice card to give to Miss Bruntford, who twisted one of her tree-trunk ankles on Friday because she decided to be standing behind me when I was **noodled**.

Isn't that nice?

I was really the one who deserved the right to nicely apologize to Bruntford, but Angeline was somehow taking credit for the apology without going to the trouble of committing the crime.

Angeline has a condition that causes her to be annoying. Doctors refer to this as **Niceism Disease** or **Nicenicity**, and we're pretty sure it has no cure. The problem is that when doctors try to cure them of it, the patients are so appreciative that they get little gift baskets for the doctors and — BAM! — now they're even nicer than they were before.

It's tragic, really.

NICENESS —

DO YOU KNOW THE RISKS?

I probably might have been sad that I had crippled somebody, but then I saw Sebastian, who, evidently, is the person filling in for Bruntford as cafeteria monitor while she's recovering.

Some people just have the sort of charm that makes you okay with crippling somebody.

Sebastian is older than we are, but young enough that it's not terribly creepy that we recognize his handsomeness. He's not old, but he's not a kid. And he's young enough that he doesn't make people call him **Mr.** This or **Mr.** That.

He has those kind of looks that makes him seem familiar somehow, like you've known him for years, even though you've never met him before.

Sebastian dresses well, and acts sophisticated. It's hard to believe that the boys in my school and Sebastian are the same species, and that one day, these **boythings** of ours could grow up to be people who care how they act around human beings, and smell less.

He didn't say much today, just sat down and started eating a regular old school lunch. I noticed right away that none of it came out of his nose. It's hard for a woman not to be **impressed** by that on some level.

I waited for Sebastian to look over at our table so that I could smile in a friendly and pretty way. When the opportunity presented itself, I smiled at him twice, just in case the first smile didn't work.

It wasn't until later that I realized that, while one smile is pleasant, that same smile performed twice in a row looks more threatening than smiley, and even the **teensiest-weensiest** bit completely insane. Turns out you just can't smile twice.

Tomorrow. It will go better tomorrow. No double-smiling tomorrow.

ONCE IS BEST

17

Dear Dumb Diary,

Mrs. Avon, my language arts teacher, is on **another** poetry kick. I've come to understand that poetry is the art of very carefully not getting to the point.

It's hard for me to believe that a whole kind of writing developed around this. Then again, I also have a hard time understanding why there are still real kings and queens in the world, but for some reason, no **jacks**.

This is our son. He wants to be an 8 or a 9 when he grows up.

Anyway, Mrs. Avon wants us to find opportunities to write little poems all month. If you ask me, I think that we should be moving away from poetry to other important literary forms, like **bumper stickers.**

I really feel that bumper stickers are the future of literature, because some of my friends won't read anything much longer than that.

I'll bet I could write a whole movie on a bumper sticker.

THESE THINGS

LUKE'S DAD IS MOSTLY A JERK. THAT ROBOT TALKS TOO MUCH. THESE FLASHLIGHTS ARE DANGEROUS.

FIND A GOLDEN TICKET AND WIN A PRIZE. NOT REALLY. JUST KIDDING, YOU DO.

HARRY IS SUPER MAD AT THE BALD GUY IN THE BLACK DRESS. HEY, SNAKES CAN TALK.

After language arts, we had lunch. It's a well-known fact that the teachers and other adults at my school use their lunch hour to hide from us and renew their energy to handle the remainder of the day. (From the smell of it, they use coffee and some kind of mushroom-beef casserole to do it.)

But since Sebastian is the current lunchroom monitor, they make him interact with us during that time. He actually **stopped by** our table at lunch today and handsomely said hello to all of us.

He has a way of being very polite without acting like some elderly great-aunt, and it makes you feel as though you should be polite back.

Even Isabella noticed it. When he said hello to her, I detected her **most sophisticated grunt** in response.

Pinsetti and Hudson were there, and Yolanda may have been there, but if so, she was too dainty for me to remember. Angeline was still in the lunch line, so I was clearly the **most lovely** girl at the table — in part because Isabella was trying to get a pudding container open with her teeth, and in part because I had successfully opened my pudding container with just my lovely hands and I was preparing to enjoy it with a plastic spoon that really highlighted the loveliness of my lovely hands.

Hate if you want to, but the girl **knows** how to handle a pudding spoon.

It's like a Utensil BALLET!

I need a bejeweled spoon or some bejeweled pudding

I was careful to perform just **one** smile at Sebastian this time, which I think is a good way to assure somebody that you are not a freak. **Not Being A Freak** is a good foundation for a friendship.

I also offered him some pudding, which was generous, and generosity is another good foundation for a friendship.

I realize now that my offer was not accompanied by any words, but consisted more of just holding the pudding up toward him, and that he may have not interpreted that as an offer, but maybe more as somebody — let's say an imbecile — wordlessly communicating something like, "Lookit, mister, I gots a pudding. I gots one. It's here. Yuh see?"

Sebastian smiled and walked away. If Isabella hadn't been so busy trying to spit out little pieces of the foil lid from her pudding cup, I'm sure that she could have helped out with a little charm. Not everybody sees it, but she really is very charming when she's not **gnawing** a dessert open.

 ♥ *Isabella's More Charminger Moments* ♥

Fed duck once. Demanded very little in return.

Took cookies to the Retirement Home at Christmas. Offered them at affordable prices.

Confessed to something.

I mean SOMEDAY she will. I just know it.

Someday

23

Dear Dumb Diary,

Handsomeness can do a lot of things, but it can't make meat loaf go away.

Lunch today was meat loaf again, as it is every Thursday. As we sat down to deal with it, Sebastian walked past. This time, I knew **exactly** what to do. I pointed at my meat loaf and offered a critical observation about its quality.

"Bleggh. Am I right?" I said, adding cleverly, "Uck."

It was the type of thing that any handsome substitute lunchroom monitor should have responded favorably to.

"Erk," you might expect him to respond. But he didn't. He just eyeballed me as if I was a twice-smiler or pudding-thruster and kept walking.

Then Angeline did the **most horrible** thing.

C'MON THIS ISN'T WEIRD

UCK

She used some sort of otherworldly power, such as you might see in a vampire, or a demon cobra, or an **annoying blond demon nice vampire cobra**, and she spoke right to him, as if she knew him or something.

"Hi, Sebastian. Would you like to join us for lunch?" she asked nicely.

He stopped, smiled, and did the most amazing thing back.

"Yes, I would, thank you," he said nicely, sitting down.

SERIOUSLY, WHAT THE HECK WAS THAT??

I am not leaving **anything** out here, Dumb Diary. It was that simple. She asked nicely, he sat nicely. Isabella was so surprised that she let a Tater Tot fall from her mouth. (Pinsetti let several fall from his, but no one batted an eye at that.)

Sebastian was **MY** discovery. I'm the one who's been putting in the time to make contact with him. I baited the hook, dropped it in the water, and now look who reels it in. And I don't even like fishing, Angeline. It's very rude to make me use it as an example.

I try and try to be friends with Angeline, and every single time, she has to do something just to annoy me, like have a nice personality.

Thanks A LOT, Angeline.

I would have much rathered some kind of princess example.

Anyway, Sebastian made conversation, and I did, too. I even made sure to use words and to keep my facial expressions to the normal number. (The **normal number** is one per expression, by the way.)

Isabella didn't contribute much, except when she started talking about her Grandma's infected foot. It's really a pretty interesting story, full of unusual bacon-grease ointments and a surprise ending, where we frightened her grandma badly with a scary face I drew on the foot while she was sleeping.

It was clear that the story was disturbing Sebastian somewhat, and Angeline changed the subject abruptly to some movie she saw and how much she liked the actress in it.

Hey, I remember what Yolanda looks like but she might be bigger than this.

"She really is a *delicate and well-mannered creature of grace,* isn't she?" Sebastian said about the actress. "So poised and charming."

It was such a beautiful thing to say that I **horked** a little. In fact, I almost horked meat loaf out of my esophagus. (Beautiful words of this intensity can affect one's esophagus, you know.)

I'm not going to give you the exact scientific definition of horking right now. It's a medical thing. Instead, here's an X-ray showing how it works:

① Beauty comes in through eyes

② Or through the EARS

③ THIS TRIGGERS THE HORK ORGAN

④ THIS CAUSES HORKAGE TO OCCUR.

Who in history has ever been called a *delicate and well-mannered creature of grace?* I was swept away for a moment, and realized that if people thought of me as a *delicate and well-mannered creature of grace* I would just die. In a good way. And I realized I want that more than anything now, more even than those **other** things I want more than anything. (To be called that, I mean. Not to die.)

I stared at Sebastian for a moment, trying to make him drown in my eyes.

"That actress kind of reminds me of you . . ." he said, making my graceful spirit spread its wings and soar.

". . . Angeline," he finished, making my graceful spirit slam into the side of a **fertilizer factory**.

SPLAT

Yeah. That's right. He was talking to ANGELINE.

Why? Just because she was all mannerly and charming about asking him to join us?

Well, *I* could have asked him to join us.

Or just because she always puts her napkin in her lap before she eats lunch?

Well, *I* could have put a napkin in my lap.

Just because she's graceful and poised and delicate and nice?

Well, *I* could have put a napkin in my lap.

DROP!

(Graceful birds

Graceful music

And I could do it MUCH more gracefully if I felt like it...

You mark my words, Angeline. I WILL BE KNOWN, FAR AND WIDE, AS A *delicate and well-mannered creature of grace,* YOU BUTTFACED BUTT.

Oh my gosh. I think I feel a poem coming on for Mrs. Avon's class:

You're pretty as a picture,
So lovely to us all.
And like a pretty picture,
We should hang you in the hall.

FRIDAY 06

Dear Dumb Diary,

Today in class, Hudson and I worked on our social-studies report. Even though he is the eighth-cutest boy in my grade, Hudson also suffers from the condition of being male, and so he wanted to do a report where we compare how other cultures go to the toilet. If I couldn't get behind that, he was also willing to do the report on how people from other countries **punch one another in the face.** He gave me the example that, even though we might punch people in a fisty way, people from other lands might use karate chops. Or friendly people might use finger flicks or slaps.

I told him that slaps are not in any way friendly, and offered to get Isabella to demonstrate one of her *special* slaps to him. After receiving one of these slaps, the recipient can taste nothing but Isabella's palm for about four days.

Hudson's Dream would be if we discovered some kind of foreign violent toilet.

Hudson finally agreed with my idea that we could focus on **manners** for our project, which I think is exactly what one might decide when partnered with a *delicate and well-mannered creature of grace.*

I also knew that manners would be a great report subject because I have to believe that most of the world is doing manners **all wrong**. We can spend a lot of time on that, including some really excellent charts to illustrate their ignorance.

Also, I believe my research is going to lead to some important rule about manners that proves that asking somebody to join you for lunch and being all diligent about putting a napkin in your lap means you're a pig, **NOT** a *delicate and well-mannered creature of grace.*

Doesn't a Napkin in the LAP indicate that you plan to eat like this?

DRoooOoL

Isabella said that she and **Yolanda the Dainty** are doing their report on marriage practices around the world, which is obviously a topic selected by Yolanda. Isabella will never get married, because it would imply that she would be required to share her cake with another person right afterward.

At least Isabella was prepared for class today with a sharpened pencil, which represents a pretty big accomplishment for her. The last time Isabella was prepared like that was back in second grade, when our class was visited by a guy that made balloon animals — an angry, yelly guy who ironically was called Pops.

I think Yolanda is going to be pleasantly surprised by the amount of work Isabella will **nearly** do on this report.

Angeline and Pinsetti are doing their report on how other cultures view us, which I suspect Angeline likes because it will give her additional chances to look in a mirror, and Pinsetti likes because it will give him additional chances to look at himself in a mirror making **gross faces**.

WHO LIKES MIRRORS THE MOST?

The VERY BEAUTIFUL?

The VERY ANNOYING?

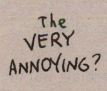

c'mon. Is there really a Difference?

Dear Dumb Diary,

Aunt Carol is a lot of fun in so many ways. None of those are coming to mind right now.

She called up to tell me she was coming over today first thing, to make me take flowers to Bruntford because the two of them are kind of friends, and I am kind of responsible for Bruntford's ankle, which is kind of injured because she is kind of gigantic.

When Aunt Carol showed up, she'd brought Angeline with her, which suddenly made it clear that this whole **let's-take-flowers-to-the-mean-old-mastodon** thing was **really Angeline's** idea.

My Aunt Carol is nice and everything, but my mom is her sister and Mom's told me **plenty** of stories about Aunt Carol.

I always forget the difference...

Is this a Mammoth or a Mastadon?

One time, when my mom and dad were just dating, he came over to pick her up. While he was waiting for my mom to get ready, Aunt Carol quietly told my dad that my mom had this terrible digestive disorder, but he shouldn't say anything because it would really, really embarrass her.

And earlier, she had told my mom that a friend of hers knew my dad, and that my dad had the **same** awful digestive disorder, but not to mention it to him because he'd be so embarrassed.

Before they left for the evening, Aunt Carol slipped a four-day-old egg-salad sandwich into the bottom of my mom's purse. They spent the entire evening thinking the other one was making that smell.

See? Aunt Carol is nice, but not as annoyingly nice as Angeline.

Back to me. Before Aunt Carol and Angeline arrived, I had looked up different flowers online to see if I could find some way that they relate to manners. I figured that if Aunt Carol was making me do this **nice stupid thing**, maybe I could pick up some little fact to use for my social-studies report.

Roses and daisies were out, because those are typically reserved for love. Some flowers, like lilies, are often used at funerals, so Bruntford would probably only appreciate those if she was dead.

For inspiration, I tried to think of the flower she most reminded me of, but it's the one that's spelled differently and is sold in five-pound bags.

Fortunately, Aunt Carol had picked up a little assorted bouquet that didn't mean anything, so that was a relief.

I talked Isabella into going along with us, because it meant we could actually look inside Bruntford's house and see if she really had a tire swing and lived only on bananas, like that rumor we started that one time.

Dumb Diary, we were **not prepared** for what we saw.

Sorry you were maimed!

At least it looked funny!

Aunt Carol wasn't crazy about my GET-WELL CARD.

Bruntford's house is beautiful, and big. **It is magnificent.** It's wonderfully decorated — and as difficult as that is to understand, Isabella had some thoughts on the matter instantly.

"Are you watching this house for somebody on vacation?" she asked Bruntford as I handed over the meaningless bouquet and the get-well card I'd made her.

expensive painting

expensive pillow

expensive chair

expensive bandage

Bruntford laughed a little, which made some of the petals fall off one of the flowers.

"My husband and I bought this house long ago and raised our son here. But Mr. Bruntford is no longer with us, I'm afraid."

"Left you, huh?" Isabella asked helpfully. "Younger woman?" She was charitably trying to spare Bruntford the embarrassment of just coming out and admitting it herself.

"He passed away," Angeline said in an angry whisper.

Aunt Carol gave Isabella a little jab with her elbow to correct her manners. You know, because nothing teaches politeness like an elbow jab.

"So, being a **Cafeteria Monitor** pays pretty well, huh?" Isabella asked.

Miss Bruntford's jiggly jowls parted enough for a smile to squeeze out from between them.

"Not at all," she said. "But Mr. Bruntford did quite well. He was already a success when we met."

Isabella eyed her and nodded with approval.

JAB

Seriously, Aunt Carol, Isabella can't feel anything softer than a flying sidekick

On the way home, I asked Aunt Carol why Miss Bruntford goes by *Miss* Bruntford instead of *Mrs.* Bruntford.

Angeline said it was probably to let guys know she's available, which made us all laugh pretty hard as well as become sick.

Aunt Carol said that Bruntford could use any title she wanted: Miss, Mrs., Ms. Whatever.

Personally, I might like to use Ms. one day. It will keep my private life private, and it will make the person talking to me **sound like a bee.**

Proper Ways to Address...

NOT MARRIED	MARRIED	UNKNOWN
Miss	*Mrs.*	*Ms.*

MARRIED TWICE	MARRIED 4 TIMES	MARRIED TO A SNAKE
Mrsrs.	*Mrsrsrsrs.*	*Missssssss*

Dear Dumb Diary,

Isabella came over to work on homework today. Mom made us lunch, which we ate anyway, and we dug into the homework for about fifteen minutes before we took a well-earned break for seven hours to do other stuff.

During that time, Isabella asked me to do something with her hair.

This kind of thing is often a **trap**. You do something to her hair, and then she offers to do something to yours, and what she does begins with spray paint and ends with the emergency room.

With Isabella, it's best to know **exactly** what you're agreeing to.

Oh, Mom,

even FOOD hates what you do to it.

So after my mom looked over the terms of our arrangement and Isabella signed it, I went to work on her hair.

She remained strangely calm throughout the process. When we were done, I think I had really done wonders for her. She looked essentially like a girl from many angles.

She didn't even make me change her hair back when she saw it.

"How long will it stay like this?" she asked. "You know, *female-looking*."

I told her only until she messed it up or slept on it, of course.

Isabella checked her phone and said that she had a fight scheduled with one of her mean older brothers later on, so I would need to fix her hair again in the morning, before school.

GIRLISH SHEEN

HIGHLY GIRLISTICAL TEXTURE

FEMININE FLIP

WOMANFUL CURL

She could learn to do her hair herself, but when I mentioned that she shoved me, because it upsets her stomach a bit when she hears the word **"learn."**

I understand. We all have our little medical conditions. I'm **blond intolerant**, for example. Sometimes.

MEDICAL PROBLEMS ON PARADE

OVERUNDEROXIA

SENSITIVITY TO WHICH WAY THE TOILET PAPER HANGS.

INBETWEENITIS

CONDITION THAT MAKES STUFF STICK IN YOUR TEETH ONLY WHEN YOU'RE DISCUSSING SOMETHING IMPORTANT.

DANGLEOSIS

A DISORDER THAT MAKES IT IMPOSSIBLE FOR YOU TO SLEEP WITH ANYTHING DANGLING OVER THE SIDE.

Dear Dumb Diary,

Before school, Isabella had me fix her hair in the girls' bathroom. Her hair really is quite beautiful. It's black and thick and glossy, like the majestic hair on a lion if that was black.

She had a test later, and she had written the answers on a slice of baloney in the sandwich she brought for lunch. If the teacher saw her, she could just eat the sandwich and destroy the evidence. But she wasn't thinking, and **accidentally** ate her lunch while I was doing her hair. Beauty can really make you hungry.

While she was wiping the ink off her lips, I explained why cheating is wrong. We have a test in math next week, and I encouraged her to pack a lunch you can't write on. If she brings peanut butter and jelly, I'll know I got through to her.

oh, Isabella, please don't ever start using your cleverness to do the wrong thing

TEST ANSWERS

We met in larger groups in social studies today to discuss what we had learned so far about other cultures.

Hudson and I shared that there are very few customs that are universal. Memorize which fork you use for the salad, and your host hands you a set of chopsticks. Practice eating gracefully with chopsticks, and your host serves fried chicken.

How can you ever know what to do?

The only way to avoid looking ridiculous is with my NEW multipurpose chopsticks and finger utensils.

GRACEFUL!

DIGNIFIED!

FINGERS!

Isabella and Yolanda seemed to have pretty similar findings about marriage. Brides don't always wear white, marriages don't all happen in churches, and the married couple doesn't always receive six toasters as gifts. Sometimes it's **even more** than that. (Note to Future Jamie: Consider marrying a man that works at an appliance store so it's easy to exchange all of your wedding gifts for something good.)

Angeline and Pinsetti had discovered that people in other countries actually have the nerve to think that we are doing certain things incorrectly when it comes to manners or customs. This is very impolite for them to do to another country, I say, especially when you consider that THEY'RE obviously the ones doing things wrong.

Hey, Others! There is a simple way to tell if you are doing something wrong —

I don't do it.

↖ Foreign customs at work

It looks like people just pull manners and customs out of thin air. So I'm just as qualified as anybody (but more qualified than most, **let's be honest**) to come up with some manners myself.

Jamie's Book of Etiquette

If you can't say something nice, don't say anything at all.

But if you can't do that, just whisper the mean stuff to me.

At lunch today, Isabella actually **stopped** Sebastian as he was walking past.

"Hey," she said. "Angeline said something to you the other day and you had lunch with us. Let's pretend that I'm saying that same thing now. So, how about it?"

She had him trapped.

"Please?" she added, and for the first time ever, I believed her.

"Well, okay," Sebastian said. "Thank you." And he sat down.

But Angeline couldn't just leave it at that.

"Well, this is nice," she added nicely, as if the rest of us hadn't noticed the niceness.

was Yolanda there? I don't remember

"So, we're talking now, right?" Isabella said. "About movies we don't really care about or things like that, right? **Polite junk**."

Sebastian seemed a little uncomfortable and looked around the table, locking eyes, one at a time, with Isabella, Angeline, Pinsetti, Hudson, and me. Yolanda may have been there, too, but I don't remember.

"You're classy, Sebastian," Isabella went on. "Bet you've been in a lot of limousines, huh?"

"Er, I haven't really." He changed the subject. "Hey, I know. Why don't you tell me what you guys are doing in your classes right now?"

"Manners and customs. Things like that," Pinsetti said. "Thank you."

Pinsetti's awkward manners, on top of Isabella's clumsy invitation and line of questioning, had Sebastian looking as uncomfortable as a snowman in a tanning bed. We all sensed it.

Isabella sometimes pinches people when things get tense this way, and as I saw her fingers begin to assume the **lobster-claw** position, I knew that somebody had to do something. Otherwise, Sebastian was going to get up and never sit down with us again, and I would never be judged as a *delicate and well-mannered creature of grace* by the one person I think is qualified to make that judgment.

Things that could Make Isabella pinch Innocent Bystanders

STRESS

SUDDEN NOISES
OR MOVEMENT

SILENCE OR
CALMNESS

"Okay, here's what we're doing," I said, not actually telling him what we were doing. "We're studying manners and customs, and we'd like your input. You're younger than the teachers, but older than we are, and we think that could help our reports."

Sebastian nodded and smiled.

"Okay, **now** I see," he said. "You're studying me, huh? Like a specimen, to see if I do anything wrong. I get it. I'll have to try to be on my best behavior."

I don't like lying to people, but they really seem to enjoy it when I do

falsehoods

Pants on fire

Pretty cool, huh? Everybody was staring at me, totally stunned. And who could blame them? I just captured us our own lunchroom monitor. He's not so old that he's going to tell us useless stuff about monocle etiquette or the right type of cape to wear to a summer opera, and he's not so young that, like Pinsetti and Hudson, he is willing to eat pudding with a comb if a spoon is unavailable. Couldn't have asked for anything better, right?

"You'll let me know if I step out of line, right, Angeline?" he said. "You're kind of the manners expert around here, I'm guessing."

Well. MAYBE I COULD HAVE ASKED FOR ONE THING BETTER.

I must Never forget to wish for **ALL** the things I really want—

6-Inch thick POP TARTS

To know a Baby named BANANAS

For Angeline to be carried off BY AN OWL

TO LIVE IN A HOUSE LIKE MY BARBIE'S

TUESDAY 10

Dear Dumb Diary,

As we were coming into the school this morning, Aunt Carol stopped me and Isabella and pulled us into the office. My Uncle Dan, who is the vice principal, was there.

"We'd like to know if you two would be willing to help plan the school dance this month," she said. "It's kind of a lot of work, and I understand if you don't —"

"We'll do it," Isabella said.

I nodded in agreement, partially because it sounded like fun and partially because Isabella was holding my head and nodding it for me.

"Sounds like fun," I said, yanking my head away from Isabella's hands.

As we started walking out of the office, Angeline walked in.

"Wow, that's pretty," she said to Aunt Carol, **spewing niceness** all over her outfit.

I clenched my teeth. I knew exactly what was going to happen.

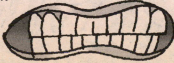

"Oh, thanks!" Aunt Carol chirped. "Say, Angeline . . ."

I could see it all happening in slow motion. Angeline had tossed a **niceness grenade**, and Aunt Carol had been hit. I made slow-motion faces and tried to escape the blast in slow motion, too, but it was no use.

Now that I think about it, when you intentionally move in slow motion like that, it looks a little **odd**.

"Angeline, would you like to help Jamie and Isabella plan the dance?" she asked nicely, trying to ignore my slow-motion thing. Aunt Carol was badly poisoned by the **niceness** Angeline had just inflicted upon her.

"Okay," Angeline nicely said. And that was nicely that.

"You're such a treasure," Aunt Carol said to Angeline.

I looked at Isabella, hoping to see one of those faces where she looks like she's plotting some sort of sabotage against somebody. But Isabella only shrugged. She might have even smiled a little. I can't be sure, so I'm going to assume she frowned and is already planning to do something awful so Angeline doesn't help us plan the dance.

Uh-oh. I think I have another poem:

Angeline, you're such a treasure,
The boys all want to marry ya.
Like all the other priceless treasures
Maybe we should bury ya.

WEDNESDAY 11

Dear Dumb Diary,

Here. Listen to this awful old terrible poem thing Mrs. Avon made us read today:

> *Shall I compare thee to a summer's day?*
> *Thou art more lovely and more temperate.*
> *Rough winds do shake the darling buds*
>   *of May,*
> *And summer's lease hath all too short*
>   *a date.*

William Shakespeare wrote it. And that's not even the entire poem. He goes on and on and on like this for fourteen lines, and here's what he was really saying:

YER PURTY. I totally mean that. REAL PURTY.

Seriously, it's all very nice, but to me, poetry seems like manners. It's designed to make things more complicated.

More and more I'm convinced that people love simple things, and my simplified bumper sticker stories are the way to go.

LIONS HAVE A BABY. A MONKEY DANGLES IT OVER A CLIFF. OH, SOME LIONS DIE.

OW. A WEIRD SPIDER BIT ME. DON'T MAKE ME USE MY WEIRD SPIDER POWERS ON YOU, YOU BIG WEIRDO.

WAIT, VOLDEMORT? IS THAT YOU? AGAIN? SAME DRESS? OK, I'LL FIGHT YOU ONE MORE TIME.

See? You just saw three movies in under a minute. This is **such** a good idea.

THURSDAY 12

Dear Dumb Diary,

Manners and meat loafs.

Today, Sebastian came and sat with us at lunch without even being asked, and we told him what we had learned in our research so far.

I shared this thing I discovered about Japan, where it's rude to stick your chopsticks straight up and down in your food.

Sebastian said that he didn't find that too surprising, since we don't stick our knife and fork straight up and down in our food, either.

"Oh yes," I said gracefully. "That wouldn't be at all well-mannered," I added like a *delicate and well-mannered creature of grace.*

I spoke so gracefully it was like I had a dove for a tongue.

That would sound graceful, right?

it would.

it would.

Isabella asked Sebastian what he could tell us about getting married, and how somebody gets proposed to, but not by a loser.

He said that he wasn't sure how that fit in with our whole manners and customs reports, but he said he thought the best way was to just try to always do your best in everything.

Isabella said that was a really great answer. A **really really** great answer. The most **wonderfullest** answer she had ever heard. Ooo. Just **wonderfullerunderfully**.

Here's my face when she said this:

except, like, way super prettier.

Hudson mentioned that he'd read an article that said there were no longer any rules or manners against burping, and that it was always considered cool to burp whenever you wanted to. He wondered if Sebastian had read the same article.

Sebastian politely responded that he had not, and Pinsetti felt as though he should add something.

"It's probably okay to do at certain times, Hudson, but nobody would ever regret it if they **didn't** burp. So, when you think about it, the best thing to do would be to —"

Then he stopped talking. He was staring at Angeline.

So now Pinsetti is some kind of PROFESSOR of BURPS

Angeline had stuck her knife and fork straight up and down in her meat loaf.

We all just paused for a moment, not knowing how to react.

Until Sebastian reacted for us.

"Well done, Angeline! Nice of you to illustrate the point. See why we don't do that? It's disruptive and distracting, and it looks like Angeline is having a fight with her meal. Well done, Angeline."

OOOOOOOOOH yes. Well done, Angeline. It's SOOOOO splendid how you can do something rude and it is interpreted as something nice. (I'm clapping very slowly right now.)

So nice. So very nice. So exquisitely nice. So jerkfully nice. So turdtastically nice.

So so so so so so so nice.

FRIDAY 13

Dear Dumb Diary,

Isabella has been making me do her hair in the girls' bathroom every single morning before school starts. This morning, while I was working on it, we came up with a few ideas for **dance themes**.

The ☆ Koala ☆ Evening ☆ of Fantasy

Girls wear elegant koala-Ear Hairdos.
Boys wear sophisticated kangaroo-tuxedos.
Guests trade very interesting koala facts.
Guests drink cola because it sounds like koala.
Everybody receives a live koala.

DANCE-FU
spectacular

A MARTIAL ARTS—THEMED DANCE WHERE EVERYBODY FIGHTS TO MUSIC. (I KNOW THIS WON'T HAPPEN, BUT ISABELLA WANTED ME TO WRITE IT DOWN.)

SQUVRSH

BROWNTOPIA

Join us for a Science-Fiction themed dance where we journey to a distant perfect planet where everybody is a Brunette. (All participants must dye hair)

The
Unicorn Princess
Fabutastical

A lovely evening of prettiness where everybody fights to music. (I know, I know, but she wanted this one too.)

SQUVRSH

At some point, Angeline walked in and stuck her big fat nose into our ideas and didn't really like any of them, which was bad enough, but her nose is also not big or fat and that makes it **worse**.

They have a lot of rules at our school against mean language, but it's pretty clear that the rule makers never had to deal with somebody's not-big and not-fat nose in their business.

We asked Angeline if she had any better ideas. Here's what she came up with:

A DANCE

People show up and dance, then leave.

A different Dance

People show up and then leave. In between, they dance.

A TOTALLY DIFFERENT DANCE

People leave. But before that, they DANCE. Before that, they show up. Okay, Angeline isn't even trying.

Jamie's Book of Etiquette

Always hold the door open for people

Unless they are one of those rotten little turds that never says thanks.

Then you can do whatever you want.

SATURDAY 14

Dear Dumb Diary,

My mom let me call Emmily today for dance-planning ideas. You remember our friend Emmily, don't you, Dumb Diary? She's very sweet but isn't exactly — what's the polite way to say this? — **as smart as a mammal.**

But she does live kind of far away now, and I thought that maybe the dances they had at her school were exotic and unusual and I could get some ideas from her.

It's always good news when you call Emmily and it's the phone she answers.

Here's how the call went:

Me: Hi, this is Jamie. Is Emmily there?

Emmily: Jamie's not here.

Me: No, Emmily. I'm Jamie. I was calling for you. How are you?

Emmily: OH! I see. This is Emmily.

Me: Yeah. Listen, Emmily, has your school had any dances this year?

Emmily: Yeah.

Me: Was there a theme?

Emmily: Dancing. The theme was dancing.

Me: Did they have any special decorations or special snacks or anything that kind of tied it all together?

Emmily: They're not allowed to tie us together, Jamie. That would be wrong. Use your head, girl! (*A full thirty seconds of goose-like laughter.*)

Me: It was nice talking to you, Emm. Talk to you soon. Bye.

Emmily: Bye, Angeline.

69

Emmily is good and kind,
She has a loving heart.
Emmily is sweet as pie,
And almost half as smart.

SUNDAY 15

Dear Dumb Diary,

I couldn't bring myself to work on my social-studies report today, even though I knew I should.

Why does that happen? Sometimes I'll look at my messy room, or a pile of homework, or the ocean of dog turds in the backyard I'm supposed to pick up, and I'll know that I **HAVE** to do something about it. I'm going to get in trouble if I don't, and I know **exactly** what to do, but I don't.

Then I know that I should feel bad about that, but I don't want to feel bad, either, so I don't. There are a lot of forces at work here, trying to make me do the right thing, but I don't do them.

People don't appreciate how much willpower it takes to do the **wrong** thing.

I'll try to summarize it in a poem:

Procrastination is a thing
That you should never do
Because it only

Dear Dumb Diary,

I had to do Isabella's hair **AGAIN** this morning, and she was rude enough to time how long it was taking me.

"Jamie, you know that my dad makes a lot of money, right?" she said.

Surprisingly, that's not the most ridiculous thing she's ever asked me. . . .

But it's up there.

See, I **KNOW** Isabella's family isn't rich. Her dad doesn't make any more money than my dad. And Isabella **KNOWS** that I know that, but just because something is a fact doesn't always mean much to Isabella.

"Yeah. I forgot to tell you," she said. "He makes, like, a whole lot of money now, and if that gets around, I don't really mind. It's a whole lot of money. Who do you think is the **richest** kid in our school?"

I told her that I used to assume it was Angeline, but now I know that she's far from rich. So I have no idea who it is.

Then Isabella began to smear on her precious ChocoMint Lip Smacker.

"Does it look like I'm wearing fancy lipstick?" she asked. She had put it on really thick.

"It looks more like you made out with a glazed donut," I said, and wiped most of it off.

It was still an awful lot of balm. She must be expecting some kind of major chapping.

We met in groups again today in social studies so we could compare our progress. Mr. Smith came around and listened in with his grouchy face and crazy toupee.

Don't look at it. Don't look at it.

Pinsetti and Angeline had a bunch of material about how other cultures think our food is gross, or how the way we dress is awful, or that our behavior is all wrong.

It's like no matter what you do, others **don't**, but they should.

Here's a useful chart I prepared to show you how the entire world is set up against you.

YOUR FAVORITE STUFF	WHAT OTHERS PROBABLY THINK ABOUT IT
YOUR FAVORITE FOOD	UNPLEASANT AND POISONOUS
YOUR VERY COMFORTABLE SOCKS	PAINFUL TO WEAR. POSSIBLY DEMONIC.
A NICE GLASS OF WATER	DROWNING HAZARD

Yolanda and Isabella didn't have very much information to share, and I could tell by looking at their dainty notes that Isabella hadn't contributed anything to the report.

Mr. Smith noticed it, too, and asked Isabella what she personally had learned about marriage around the world.

"I'm still working on that, Mr. Smith," she said. "Nice tie."

They say you always remember where you were or what you were doing the first time you experience an earthquake, or a tornado, or, I don't know, some other rare natural event. A penguin mauling, let's say.

Me? I'll always remember the time Isabella complimented a teacher.

Okay, I've never seen one, but I'd remember it.

"Oh," Mr. Smith said, his grouchy face twisting into a huge smile. "Thanks. You know, my wife gave this to me. I get more compliments on this tie. . . ."

And he stood up and moved on to the next group.

I stared at Isabella, and **she knew** I was staring. She wanted to look over at me and grin, I could tell, but she didn't. It took every muscle in her whole muscular face, but she controlled it, and later on she wouldn't even talk about it.

GGNNGG

VRRRF

GRUNNT

NNNNG

When your friend flexes her face

TUESDAY 17

Dear Dumb Diary,

Word is out that we're planning the dance, so we've received a lot of suggestions.

Spitty Elizabeth suggested an underwater theme. (Probably because of her familiarity with moisture.)

Margaret, the pencil chewer, suggested a ninja theme. (Thinking of those delicious numchucks no doubt.)

Vicki, the copier of everybody, suggested an underwater ninja theme, and then argued that she didn't copy off anybody. **NOTE TO COPIERS: WE KNOW, OKAY.**

And then Pinsetti came over to make a suggestion.

SERIOUSLY, PEOPLE, I don't want you to get the wrong idea.

And when you DO GET A WRONG IDEA, I don't want to hear it, either.

"How about a fancy theme? Where everybody dresses up and acts fancy and everything like that?" he suggested. "Polite underwear, nice snacks that you can't blow out your nose. All that really fancy stuff."

This from the guy with the nostril noodle. The guy with thirty-seven words for diarrhea. (Only, like, nine of them are even funny.) The guy who once ate a beetle off an old sandwich on an old shoe. True, this was years ago, and there was a double dare involved, but still.

**This** is the guy who wants a fancy dance?

I prepared a laugh to discharge directly into the middle of his face just as Isabella spoke up.

"That's a good idea, Mike," she said, doubling her previous record for compliments given in a month.

Isabella wanted a fancy dance, too.

Then she turned to me.

"Oh, Jamie. Don't worry about that seven hundred dollars you owe me. You don't have to pay me back."

WHAT?

No hair spray for Isabella tomorrow. I'm afraid that she may have accidentally inhaled some.

WEDNESDAY 18

Dear Dumb Diary,

So at lunch today, Isabella went and asked Angeline to tell us everything we needed for a fancy dance. We didn't need her help, of course, but Isabella can be a little impulsive. Before Angeline could answer, Hudson butted in.

"Whose idea was this?" he demanded.

Pinsetti was giving us the **tiniest frantic secret head shakes**, indicating that we shouldn't say that it had been him.

"It was Angeline's idea," Isabella said.

Angeline started to say that it wasn't, but she saw Pinsetti's panic and decided to reluctantly go along with it. You know, because she's **nice**.

"Yeah. It. Was. My. Idea," she said, and Hudson calmed down because eighty pounds of radiant pure blond hair just has that effect on Hudson, I guess.

Isabella said that Angeline should make a list of all the **fancy things** we need for a fancy dance, like fancy snacks, and fancy signs, and fancy balloons.

"Is there, like, some kind of fancy air that fancy people use in their balloons?" Isabella asked her.

"You mean like helium?" Angeline said unpleasantly.

"Helium **is** just fancy air, isn't it?" Isabella said, as though some secret balloon scam had just been revealed to her.

I suppose all of this fancy dance stuff has something to do with customs and manners, and that means we can all use it in our reports. We'd *better* be able to use it in our reports. I'm sacrificing my *Koala Evening of Fantasy* theme for this.

The delicacy!
The grace!
→

Dances always require a few adult chaperones, so I asked Sebastian if he'd like to be a chaperone for our fancy dance since he's so **sophisticated** and junk.

I didn't want to leave Yolanda out of our dance planning — since she's doing the report with Isabella, she's kind of a temporary friend now. I asked her if she could review everything for **daintiness**.

She looked at me as if I had just produced a nose noodle of my own, but I'm sure she gets what I mean.

C'mon, Yolanda— It's not that tough...

NOT DAINTY	DAINTY	TOO DAINTY
punch served in old BEAN CANS	punch served in small punch glasses	punch served in the cupped hands of a baby
Balloons made of inflated Paper Bags	Balloons made of Balloon material	Balloons made of embroidered silk
music provided by ape banging on dirty Bucket	music provided by DJ	music provided by princess tapping on golden Bucket

THURSDAY 19

Dear Dumb Diary,

Meat loaf again, but without Bruntford around to make sure that you choke down every crumb, it's not so bad. Yup, there's nothing that improves school meat loaf like not eating it.

Pinsetti **wore a tie** to school today, and actually **pulled out a chair** for Angeline when she sat down.

This caused a huge conflict in my feelings about him.

My first assumption, of course, was that he was wearing a tie because somebody had tied it around him, and he wasn't able to get it off. (Stuff like that happens to my dog, Stinker, all the time.) The next thought I had was that he was going to pull the chair away when Angeline sat down.

But Angeline was seated safely, and the tie was only partially stupid-looking, and since it would be very hard for Pinsetti to seem any grosser, I had to admit that all of this was kind of an improvement.

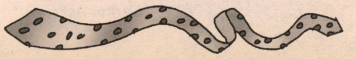

This is the **advantage** the gross have over the rest of us. Almost anything makes them look better.

OGRE

+

STYLISH HAT

ZOMBIE MISSING HEAD

+

BUCKET WITH HAPPY FACE

ZOMBIE HEAD

+

LOVELY ORNATE BIRDCAGE

Hudson quizzed Pinsetti about the tie —
where he learned to tie it and all that — and
Pinsetti said that he just wanted to practice so that
he knew what to do for the dance.

Then Isabella said she thought it was a great
idea, and an awesome tie. (That's right, Dumb
Diary: compliments number **three** and **four**.)

I used my eyes to send Isabella a message
that said, "You are sounding like a huge weirdo."
She used her eyes to send a message back to me
saying, "What? What are you talking about?" Then I
sent her a message with my eyes that said, "You
know exactly what I'm talking about," and then I
think Isabella swore at me with her eyes.

Sebastian stopped briefly at our table and
said hello. He even commented that Pinsetti looked
"dashing" in his tie.

Then he turned to Angeline.

"What kind of knot would you say he's tied there, Angeline? A Prince Albert? A Windsor?" Sebastian stood and smiled, awaiting her expert opinion.

Angeline shrugged her shoulders.

"It's a **four-in-hand**," Hudson said.

We all looked at him, and he coughed.

"That's what Pinsetti told me it was. Right, Mike? Something like that, I think you said."

"You know all those knots?" Isabella asked Mike, clearly impressed.

"Yes, thank you," Pinsetti said, grinning.

Evidently, there is more than one way to tie a necktie...

The four-in-hand

The King Tut

The Hostage

Before he walked away, I made sure that Sebastian saw some *graceful, well-mannered, delicate* things going on over here in Jamieville.

Like, I arranged the meat loaf into adorable little teddy bear wads.

With my pinkie extended and the fork's pinkie extended as well.

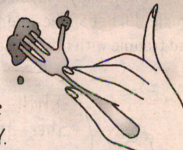

And when the meat loaf wads made me gag, I used my napkin to delicately muffle the wet, strangled sounds I gracefully made.

FRIDAY 20

Dear Dumb Diary,

> *There's just about a week to go*
> *Until our fancy dance.*
> *I think that I might wear a dress,*
> *The boys will wear some pants.*

Okay, okay. Maybe this one is a little too simple. I'll bet Shakespeare had a few days when he had trouble with his poems, too:

Shall I compare thee to a summer's day?

No. That would be way hard.

SATURDAY 21

Dear Dumb Diary,

Hudson and I needed to get together today to work on our report. I wanted him to come over, but that would technically be a date and possibly lead to an engagement. (I'm too young, Hudson, please. **Get over it.**) So I suggested we all get together as a large group, instead.

Pinsetti recommended meeting at Hudson's house, since it's kind of in the middle for all of us. So we all agreed and called Hudson this morning to let him know that he agreed, too.

That's how it's going down, Huds.

master of social situations

I had never been inside Hudson's house, although I was very familiar with the part of the front room you could see if you leaned way over and peeked in the window when nobody was home just before you fell in the bushes.

The house was very nice and quite tidy. You're never really prepared for a boy's house to be tidy. You expect everything to be wrinkly and have **cargo pockets**.

Hudson's mom set us up in their basement, and brought us orange juice and cookies. She used real glasses and real plates — not like my mom, who has actually served us sandwiches on envelopes when the dishes were dirty.

The cutlery was also dirty, so we had to cut the meat with scissors.

The group-homework strategy worked pretty well this time. It turns out that I had discovered some things about marriage that Isabella and Yolanda could use, and Angeline and Pinsetti passed along some stuff about manners that they had found.

And every time somebody felt like goofing off, there were enough other people there to keep them going. Maybe these group projects **aren't** as dumb as most of us have learned they are.

Each of us is like a brick in a house!

A house made out of, like, 5 bricks.

We even had a little time at the end to talk about the dance. Pinsetti had an idea for a game where you have to put all of the pieces of a fancy table setting into the right places. You know, like, "the salad fork goes here, the bread plate goes there." He had a printout of a complicated setting he found online.

I thought it was too hard, but Hudson said it was stupid because it was **too easy**.

"Too easy?" Pinsetti said. "Yeah, right, you couldn't —"

And before he could even finish, Hudson had scribbled a setting on a piece of paper.

pretty cute
even when
scribbling
angrily

He handed it to Angeline.

"Check it, Angeline. Is it right?" he asked.

Angeline took the paper and started to check it before a look of **anger** flashed across her face. She suddenly pushed it back at him in a way that was anything but nice.

"What makes you think I would know if this was right or not?" she said angrily.

Pinsetti checked it against the printout.

"You're right. This is all right. How did you know this?" Pinsetti asked.

Hudson made a face as though he realized that he had just been caught tossing mice on tiny crutches into a bathtub full of cats.

"I saw it in some movie once," he mumbled. "Time to go."

SUNDAY 22

Dear Dumb Diary,

Poster Time! That's right. Dances need posters, and posters need me.

Today I started drawing and decorating with such artistic fury that Dad left the kitchen twice to hack glitter out of his lungs.

Stinker and his dogdaughter, Stinkette, are dumb, and believe that all of the events occurring on a kitchen table involve food, so they will consider eating anything that falls off of it. It's the main reason I don't have Isabella help with these craft projects, because she likes to cut construction paper into convincing food shapes and feed it to them.

Still, I wish I knew somebody that could help me.

HEY, STUPID, THIS IS TURKEY

I called Angeline a few times for advice on the fanciest way to word the posters, but I'm not sure her heart was in it. I finally figured it out without her help. It's what you'd expect from a **C.O.G.** (That stands for *creature of grace*, if you're too ill-mannered and indelicate to know.)

DANCE SHMANCE CALL IT WHAT YOU WANT

THE STOP CALLING ME DANCE

JAMIE, I DON'T CARE WHAT YOU PUT ON THE POSTERS.

NO, I DON'T WANT YOU TO WRITE THAT DOWN.

MONDAY 23

Dear Dumb Diary,

Isabella asked me to lend her some earrings today, and I brought them to our morning hair session. She wanted me to bring in the most expensive-looking ones I had.

Like most *creatures of grace,* I have **many** earrings. They fall into four main categories:

- I will never wear these.
- I will probably never wear these.
- I might wear these some time, I don't know. Probably not.
- I wear these three pairs of earrings.

MY NECKLACES FALL INTO JUST TWO CATEGORIES

I MIGHT WEAR ONE OF THESE IF I EVER GET THEM UNTANGLED

WHAT THE HECK IS THIS THING?

I'd brought a big pair of sparkly earrings that I think could be mistaken for **real jewels** if you didn't look closely and had never seen a real jewel before.

Isabella put them on, and as I was brushing her hair, I realized that Isabella doesn't have pierced ears.

Well, she *didn't used to have* pierced ears.

"I just pushed them through my earlobes. That's what you do, right?" she said.

I worried about her getting an infection, but only for a second. Isabella's immune system is pretty tough. Diseases wash their hands after they come in contact with her.

What's wrong, Flu?

I touched Isabella and I've been throwing up germs all night.

After her hair was done, Isabella helped me hang posters until she saw Pinsetti coming down the hall in his tie, again. Then she pretended that she couldn't reach high enough.

"Mike, could you help us with this?" she asked ~~nicely~~ grossly.

"Thank you," Pinsetti said ~~nicely~~ weirdly, and helped.

After he was gone, I inspected her ears to see if the earring posts had penetrated into her skull and damaged her brain.

"Isabella, why are you being so nice?" I asked her.

"Shut up. Because I am," she said back with a smile and a **very hard shove**.

Aww. Wook at wittle Isabella! What could be more adorable than pretending to be helpless?

PWEASE HELP WITTLE ME

Um... ANYTHING.

Jamie's Book of Etiquette

Always cover your mouth when you sneeze.

Or cough. Or burp.

You know, we wouldn't mind if some of you just kept it covered all the time.

TUESDAY 24

Dear Dumb Diary,

Today Isabella asked Angeline for some ideas for fancy activities for the dance. There is a very good chance that Yolanda was standing there as well, but truthfully, I don't remember.

"What would be good?" I asked.

"How about a spitting contest?" Angeline offered. "To see who could spit the farthest. Maybe we could use olive pits or raisins. Maybe just pure spit."

She was trying to appear helpful, but her answer made it clear that she was annoyed, which was so peculiar because I was being so nice.

Oh. My. Gosh. It happened.

I truly **AM** a *delicate and well-mannered creature of grace.* I've become **SO** nice that I'm actually **annoying the nice people.**

I'm like a mosquito that gave another mosquito malaria.

a
(pretty)
mosquito

Dear Dumb Diary,

> *A graceful girl,*
> *With perfect manners,*
> *Knows just the fork*
> *To eat bananners,*
> *And where the dinner napkin goes,*
> *And knows it snot*
> *For snot from nose.*

Handsome princes approve of sophisticated fork selection.

You know, Mrs. Avon, I think I may be coming around on the poetry obsession of yours. It really **does** convey beautiful things in a way that just coming right out and saying it doesn't.

THURSDAY 26

Dear Dumb Diary,

Our reports are due tomorrow, so today was the last time we'd be able to get more insight from Sebastian.

I sat very *delicately* at the lunch table, and spoke very *gracefully*, and used my manners very *welly*.

I cleverly pushed the conversation toward that what's-her-name movie star that he said was a *delicate and well-mannered* blah blah blah.

"Oh yes, *her*," Sebastian said with, let's face it, a little **too** much niceness.

"She's probably not, you know, the **ONLY** person in the world like that," I said with a delicacy that would totally kick her delicacy in its face.

"I'm sure you're right," he said.

"That's the kind of thing you might notice about someone anyplace," I hinted well-manneredly.

"I don't really . . ." His voice trailed off.

I knew this conversation was beginning to go badly. Any moment, Isabella would pinch somebody or Angeline would change the subject.

Come on, Sebastian. Did I have to spell it out?

I cleared my throat. "Who at this table, right now, would you say is the most *delicate and well-mannered creature of grace?*"

"Before you answer that, Sebastian," Angeline said, "I have one thing I'd like to say."

Angeline. I knew she would change the subject.

I suppose Mrs. Shakespeare will always remember where she was the exact moment that William Shakespeare wouldn't shut up about how pretty she was.

And the ninja Pilgrims will always remember where they were the exact moment one of them karate-chopped Plymouth Rock in half.

And we will always remember where we were at the **exact moment** when Angeline looked Sebastian right in the eye and did a fart.

HORRIBLE NOISE.

Hudson laughed.

Pinsetti was confused.

I gasped (being careful not to **inhale** as I did).

Isabella kept eating.

Yolanda maybe did something, but I can't remember what it was.

Sebastian stood up, looking uncomfortable.

"I just remembered that I was supposed to meet somebody," he stammered.

"Wait, wait." I said. "The *creature of grace* and junk. Who is it?"

Sebastian looked at Angeline, who returned his gaze flatly, chewing with her mouth open. His eyes went around our table, stopping on each person, except maybe Yolanda. I can't remember for sure if she was even there.

Pinsetti adjusted his tie.

"Mike," Sebastian said hurriedly. "It's Mike."

Then he darted off.

Isabella smiled at Pinsetti.

"That's who I would have picked," she said. "Save a dance for me tomorrow night."

Pinsetti sat up straighter and beamed. He suddenly became more handsome, less gross, and as strange as it is to admit, he might have been **more** than just a creature. He might have actually been a *creature of grace.*

YEAH, that's great and EVERYTHING, But if it hadn't been for Angeline's **GROSSNESS** he probably would have SAID **ME**

They all got up, leaving me and Angeline alone at the lunch table. She straightened up and grinned. "How gross was that?"

"On a scale of one to yuck," I said, "I'd give it a nine."

She laughed. "I shouldn't have done it."

"There are no take backs on a fart," I said. Then I paused and said it again slower, so that the full wisdom of what I was saying sunk in. It's the kind of **wise phrase** you see carved on monuments.

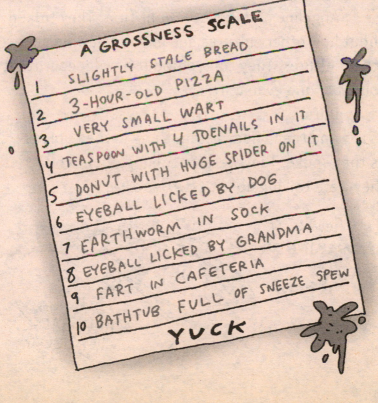

A GROSSNESS SCALE

1 SLIGHTLY STALE BREAD
2 3-HOUR-OLD PIZZA
3 VERY SMALL WART
4 TEASPOON WITH 4 TOENAILS IN IT
5 DONUT WITH HUGE SPIDER ON IT
6 EYEBALL LICKED BY DOG
7 EARTHWORM IN SOCK
8 EYEBALL LICKED BY GRANDMA
9 FART IN CAFETERIA
10 BATHTUB FULL OF SNEEZE SPEW
YUCK

FRIDAY 27

Dear Dumb Diary,

Good news and bad news.

The bad news is that I **woke up** this morning.

Today was the day we had to give the oral part of our report to the whole social-studies class . . . and when I realized the risk of group projects.

Angeline and Pinsetti went first. They talked about how other cultures see us, and how we see other cultures. They talked about how inaccurate it could be, and even unfair.

Unfair.

And then I heard something in their voices as they spoke. They weren't talking about countries. They were talking about *themselves*.

BEWARE OF WAKING UP

It's how ALL BAD DAYS Begin

See, Pinsetti has always been the definition of **gross**. And he seemed okay with it. He might have even liked it. But when he saw Sebastian's effect on everybody, I'll bet that he decided he wanted to be seen differently. He wore a tie. He spoke politely. He suggested the fancy dance theme so he'd have an excuse to clean up a little and not be judged for it.

And maybe Angeline feels like the opposite. That's why she was getting so irritated about being asked for fancy-manners advice. Maybe she's sick of everybody always thinking she's **so nice**. And she's sick of people thinking she's **so fancy**. And she's sick of people thinking she's **so mannerly**.

That fart sure sounded like she was sick.

Maybe people are more complicated than we think...

It would be **SO** like people to try to mess us up that way.

Isabella and Yolanda went next. I was thinking about Angeline, and for the first time I really looked at Yolanda. Maybe she's not so dainty. She has huge, undainty feet, and crazy socks, and when she held up their poster, I saw that she actually has **MAD GLITTER** skills. I don't know how I missed all that. I was focused on the dainty, I guess.

During their presentation, Isabella talked about how important marriage is from the standpoint of the wife, especially in places where women don't have as much access to high-paying job opportunities, and sometimes those arranged marriages make a lot of sense. Mr. Smith asked her if she thought love mattered as well, and she gave him the darkest look she's given in weeks.

"Ever try to buy groceries with love?" she asked him. I swear the temperature in the room fell a few degrees. **It was good to have her back.**

Love **is** the most important thing

But Isabella doesn't think it's the **ONLY THING**

Suddenly it was clear to me where Isabella was coming from. I wanted to grab her by the shoulders and shake her, but it was Hudson's and my turn to present and shaking Isabella is kind of suicidal, anyway.

I went up to the front of the room and held up a fabulous presentation board — and made eye contact with Yolanda as I did. She nodded her head slightly, showing respect for my glitterization in the way only a fellow **glitterizer** could.

I started speaking, but Hudson jumped right in and interrupted.

Glitterizers recognize that CERTAIN SPARKLE in each others' eyes.

Although those might just be fragments of glitter. (They're often visible in nostrils, too.)

"Manners and customs are dumb," he began. "They don't do anything but make people feel like they don't belong or that they aren't good enough." He set his jaw, and turned to look at me. I saw my **entire grade** going down the drain.

"That's not true, Hudson," I fumbled. "In fact, you have perfect manners yourself." I grinned at Mr. Smith (without looking at his untrue hair), trying to save my grade.

Hudson scoffed.

"It's a lot of work. Too much work," he groaned. "Eat with whatever fork you want. Eat with your hands if you want to. It's your food, right? Elbows on the table, talk with your mouth full. What difference does it make? Just to make us look better than others?"

There was a surprising amount of anger bubbling up out of Hudson.

And for a moment, I didn't know what to say. I kind of agreed with him.

I'd spent four weeks on this project, and it was **crashing down** around me.

RUN! The Grades are falling!!

Just then, a small, dainty, clean voice rang out.

"Manners exist so we can stand each other," Yolanda said.

And it was suddenly clear to me.

"Yeah," I said. "Manners don't make us great. They make us tolerable. Barely tolerable to each other."

With that, Mr. Smith didn't crack a smile. Nope, he laughed so hard that his toupee shifted.

Don't look at it. Don't look at it.

"We all would be at each other's throats like dogs fighting over something that fell off the table, or we'd be doing gross things in public," I said.

Hudson looked at Angeline and held back a grin.

I went on. "It doesn't matter who you are, or where you are. All manners are supposed to do is make you bother the people around you less."

Mr. Smith asked people for examples of behavior that bothered them, and people began shouting things out.

"Not covering your mouth when you cough."

"Not saying thank you."

"Shouting things out!" shouted out Mr. Smith.

Eventually, Hudson threw up his hands and surrendered.

"You win!" he said. "They matter. Manners matter."

I realized that, to Mr. Smith, it probably looked like we had staged a debate, instead of really having one.

Now here's that **good news**: Later on, as we were leaving the class, Mr. Smith stopped me and spoke quietly.

"That was my favorite presentation all year, Miss Kelly," he said. "If ninja Pilgrims are absent from the written part of your report this time, I think you'll be very happy with your grade."

Don't look at it. Don't look at it.

Later on, we went to the dance.

It didn't turn out too bad, if I do say so myself. Lots of people came, and they even dressed up a little. Though after they were there for ten minutes, the girls took off their shoes and the boys looked like they always do.

Almost nobody could win the Arrange The Silverware game. Except **Hudson**, of course.

After he finished, Angeline walked over and moved a utensil.

"He has the oyster fork wrong. It goes on the far right," she said.

"So, you **are** fancy?" I asked.

Angeline raised an eyebrow at me. "You're not going to make me do **you know what** again, are you?"

I made a *delicate and well-mannered* face of utter disgust.

BREAD KNIFE   BREAD PLATE

DESSERT SPOON

CAKE FORK

WATER GOBLET   RED WINEGLASS   WHITE WINEGLASS

NAPKIN

SALAD FORK   DINNER FORK

DINNER KNIFE

SOUP SPOON

OYSTER FORK

TEASPOON

We stood and watched Isabella try to dance with Pinsetti. Pinsetti was very politely dancing very badly so that nobody noticed Isabella dancing merely badly. Or maybe he really is that bad.

Angeline felt that she had to explain her little audio performance at lunch yesterday. She said that she didn't like being thought of as **just** nice and polite and mannerly.

"There's more to me than that," she said. "I don't want to be seen as just a *delicate and well-mannered creature of grace.* Why would anybody want that? There's more to everyone. Like, what if everyone only thought of Yolanda as this dainty little thing? They would hardly ever notice her. They wouldn't even bother to watch her dance."

Angeline motioned to the dance floor, and Yolanda the Dainty was indeed burning up the floor with moves you could hardly call dainty. I'm an expert on dancing. How could I have **missed** that?

When the song ended, Isabella joined us. She picked up a cookie from the snack table and crammed it in her mouth, chewing it more enthusiastically than she had chewed something in weeks.

"Not bad, huh?" she said, pointing at Pinsetti. "Richest boy in the school, I bet. He'd marry me, you know, if I asked him."

Angeline choked on her punch.

"HUH?" I said.

"Yeah. That's why I've been looking so pretty. And I've been using niceness and politeness against him, you know, like Angeline does. It's like some kind of **superweapon**. People are helpless against it. Even teachers." She grinned maniacally. "I get you now, Angeline. I get you."

Angeline was shocked. "Wait. You want to marry Pinsetti?"

CHOMP
GOBBLE
SNARF
NOM
NOM
CHOMP
NARF

So nice to see

"No, no. Of course not. This was just practice. I figured if I knew how to get a rich boy to fall for me now, when I'm older, I could get a rich **man** to do the same thing."

"Is that why you wanted people to think you were rich?" I asked her.

"Yup. Because the rich stick together, like money sticks together. Hey, I think I danced out an earring."

"Good luck with that," Angeline said, and Isabella returned to the dance floor.

"Isabella isn't **really** nice," I said, relieved.

"Nope," Angeline said. "And Pinsetti's not rich. He's just doing his best to be nicer. The necktie, the manners — Isabella mistakes all that for being rich. Plus, I don't think Pinsetti has fallen for her. He just likes not grossing somebody out."

"Maybe Hudson is the richest," I said.

"What difference would it make?" Angeline said.

"None, I guess. But he **is** kind of fancy, you can't deny that."

"His parents focus a lot on manners, and that's probably why he snapped. He got tired of it. But he's not richer than any of us." She stopped and watched the people on the dance floor for a minute. "And besides, look at Isabella — people can pretend to be nice, or they can pretend not to be. I like what you said — manners just make it so we don't bother each other too much. That's pretty much all they're good for."

And now I think that's enough.

NOT BOTHERING PEOPLE ROCKS!

"Do you think that Sebastian really **is** rich?" I asked Angeline.

Before she could answer, the door to the cafeteria opened, and Bruntford hobbled in on a cane. I wondered what she was doing there.

"Well . . ." Angeline smiled. "I think he's probably doing okay." She winked as she nodded toward Bruntford.

Sebastian walked over, hugged Bruntford, and gave her a little kiss on the cheek.

"OMG!!! SEBASTIAN IS DATING BRUNTFORD!!!" I yell-whispered.

"Whattt?? Sebastian is Bruntford's **son**," Angeline said. "Everybody knows that. That's why he was filling in for her. His pictures were up at her house, for crying out loud."

Oh my gosh. I *thought* he looked familiar.

"Isabella should keep in mind that if she marries somebody just for their money, she might not like what goes along with the deal."

Oh, man. Angeline was right. Can you imagine what the kids might look like?

monocle because only Isabella wears glasses

SATURDAY 28

Dear Dumb Diary,

    I went over to Isabella's house today and was happy to learn that she is back to her normal self. The vision of Sebastian arm in arm with Bruntford shook her to her core.

    She had never really considered the power of niceness before, and said that she thinks it has some real potential, although she now sees the great risk of using niceness recklessly and ending up with Bruntford as your **mother-in-law**.

    She said that she thinks it's okay to be nice, but you have to be careful when you fake it.

Hudson emailed me a thank-you note today, too. (I guess it's that mannerly upbringing he had.) Here's what it said:

Dear Jamie —

Thanks for your hard work on our project. I might have blown it for us if you hadn't done so well in the presentation. You really had it right.

Sincerely,
Hudson

P.S. My mom would like to invite you, Isabella, Angeline, Pinsetti, and Yolanda over for dinner. She'll make her specialty — spaghetti.

I'll still be reminded of Pinsetti's nose as I eat. But it would be rude to decline the invitation, and I think that I can now imagine Pinsetti's nose as a more *delicate and well-mannered* feature of his face. Besides, if it gets really uncomfortable, I can count on Isabella to start pinching.

Oh, one other thing, Dumb Diary. You know how Shakespeare wrote that poem for his true love? I made one for mine. It's called **"Dear Dumb Diary":**

When I'm sweet,
Or when I'm yelly,
Thanks for listening,

Jamie Kelly

Do Manners Matter?

Think you've got what it takes to master manners, like Angeline, Hudson, and Pinsetti? Test your skills below!

1.) If you accidentally burp at the dinner table, you should say:
   a. "You're welcome!"
   b. "Yum. Even better the second time."
   c. "Excuse me."
   d. "Did somebody just say your name?"

2.) If a friend has food stuck in her teeth, you should:
   a. Laugh and point
   b. Tell her quietly, so she can remove it right away

c. Make up a song about it and hope she gets the point by listening to the lyrics
d. Use your hands to try and forcefully pull the food out for her

3.) At a formal dinner, your napkin goes:
   a. Tucked in your shirt like a bib
   b. On your head, folded like a fancy hat
   c. Waving in the air like a white flag when you surrender and can't eat any more
   d. In your lap

4.) When you answer the phone, you should say:
   a. "Hello, (your last name) residence!"
   b. "Yeah?"
   c. "Not you again."
   d. "Tony's Pizza, can I take your order?"

5.) When eating soup, it's most polite to:
   a. Slurp, so everyone knows you like it
   b. Place face in bowl and eat, in case your host would be offended if you lifted the bowl
   c. Eat quietly off a spoon
   d. Fold tiny boat from napkin. Place in soup to create lovely nautical scene.

Answers: 1.) c 2.) b 3.) d 4.) a 5.) c

HEY! WHATEVER YOU DO, DON'T LOOK FOR JAMIE KELLY'S NEXT **TOP SECRET** DiARY....

**DEAR DUMB DIARY YEAR TWO #3:
NOBODY'S PERFECT. I'M AS CLOSE AS IT GETS.**

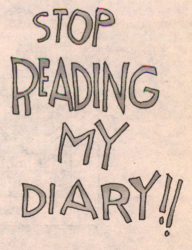

DEAR DUMB DIARY,

CAN'T GET ENOUGH OF JAMIE KELLY?
CHECK OUT HER OTHER DEAR DUMB DIARY BOOKS!

YEAR TWO:

#1: School. Hasn't This Gone On Long Enough?

WWW.SCHOLASTIC.COM/DEARDUMBDIARY

#1: Let's Pretend This Never Happened

#2: My Pants Are Haunted!

#3: Am I the Princess or the Frog?

#4: Never Do Anything, Ever

#5: Can Adults Become Human?

#6: The Problem With Here Is That It's Where I'm From

#7: Never Underestimate Your Dumbness

#8: It's Not My Fault I Know Everything

#9: That's What Friends <u>Aren't</u> For

#10: The Worst Things In Life Are Also Free

#11: Okay, So Maybe I Do Have Superpowers

#12: Me! (Just Like You, Only Better)

Our Dumb Diary: A Journal to Share

Totally Not Boring School Planner

read them all!

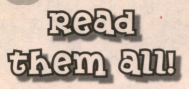

Life, Starring Me!

Callie for President

Drama Queen

I've Got a Secret

Confessions of a Bitter Secret Santa

Super Sweet 13

The Boy Next Door

The Sister Switch

Snowfall Surprise

Rumor Has It

The Sweetheart Deal

The Accidental Cheerleader

The Babysitting Wars

Star-Crossed

Accidentally
Fabulous

Accidentally
Famous

Accidentally
Fooled

Accidentally
Friends

How to Be a Girly Girl in
Just Ten Days

Ice Dreams

Juicy Gossip

Making Waves

Miss Popularity

Miss Popularity
Goes Camping

Miss Popularity
and the Best Friend Disaster

Totally Crushed

Wish You Were Here,
Liza

See You Soon,
Samantha

Miss You, Mina

Winner Takes All

About Jim Benton

Jim Benton is not a middle-school girl, but do not hold that against him. He has managed to make a living out of being funny, anyway.

He is the creator of many licensed properties, some for big kids, some for little kids, and some for grown-ups who, frankly, are probably behaving like little kids.

You may already know his properties: It's Happy Bunny™ or Just Jimmy™, and of course you already know about Dear Dumb Diary.

He's created a kids' TV series, designed clothing, and written books.

Jim Benton lives in Michigan with his spectacular wife and kids. They do not have a dog, and they especially do not have a vengeful beagle. This is his first series for Scholastic.

Jamie Kelly has no idea that Jim Benton, or you, or anybody is reading her diaries. So, please, please, please don't tell her.